The Incredible Something

Written by Danny Katz

Illustrated by Mitch Vane

sundance™

 a black dog book

Published by
Sundance Publishing
33 Boston Post Road West
Suite 440
Marlborough, MA 01752
1-800-343-8204
www.sundancepub.com

Copyright © text Danny Katz
Copyright © illustrations Mitch Vane

First published 2001 by
Pearson Education Australia Pty. Limited
95 Coventry Street
South Melbourne 3205 Australia
Exclusive United States Distribution: Sundance Publishing

Guided Reading Level I
Guided reading levels assigned by Sundance Publishing using the text characteristics
described by Fountas & Pinnell in their book *Guided Reading,* published by Heinemann.

ISBN 978-0-7608-4992-7

Printed by Nordica International Ltd.
Manufactured in Guangzhou, China
April, 2011
Nordica Job#: 03-55-11
Sundance/Newbridge PO#: 226450

Contents

Chapter One

The Smart Idea _____ 1

Chapter Two

Getting Started _____ 5

Chapter Three

Taking Shape _____ 11

Chapter Four

So Much to Do _____ 17

Chapter Five

Almost Done _____ 23

Characters

Smart Alec loves to do things her own way.

Barney Gavarney likes to help out whenever he can.

The **Henson twins** always do everything together.

Molly P. Crisp would like to be friends with Smart Alec.

Chapter One
The Smart Idea

Smart Alec had a smart idea.

She thought it might be

the smartest idea that she'd ever had.

Smart Alec was going to build
something in the front yard.
It was going to be something big.

It was going to be something great.

It was going to be

the most incredible something

anyone had ever built.

Only Alec knew how to build
the incredible something.
That's because she was Smart Alec.

Chapter Two
Getting Started

Smart Alec got some cardboard boxes.

She stacked them higher and higher.

The Henson twins came along and said,

"What are you building, Alec?"

"Something amazing," said Smart Alec.

"But the weather doesn't look very good," said the Henson twins at the same time.

"Shhhhhh! I'm trying to build this amazing something," said Smart Alec. So the Henson twins just stood and watched while Smart Alec built her amazing something.

Smart Alec got a bunch of sticks

from under the tree.

She stuck them into the cardboard boxes.

Some sticks pointed to the left.

Some sticks pointed to the right.

And one big stick at the top

pointed straight up.

Molly P. Crisp came along and said,
"What are you building, Alec?"

Smart Alec said, "Something fantastic."

"Those clouds look dark and scary," said Molly.

"Shhhhhh!" said Smart Alec.
"I'm busy building my fantastic something."

So Molly P. Crisp just stood and watched
while Smart Alec built her fantastic something.

Smart Alec went into the kitchen.

She got a spoon and some raisins

and a big piece of watermelon.

She stuck the spoon in here.

She put the raisins over there.

She stuck the watermelon on the stick

that was poking out near the top.

Chapter Three
Taking Shape

Barney Gavarney popped his head
over the fence. "What are you building, Alec?"

"I'm building something astonishing,"
said Smart Alec.

"I think a terrible storm is coming,"
said Barney.

Smart Alec said, "Shhhhhh! Can't you see
I'm building an astonishing something?"

So Barney Gavarney just watched
while she kept building
the astonishing something.

The sky was getting dark,

and the wind was starting to blow.

The raisins were rolling around,

and the sticks were shaking.

The incredible something

was wobbling back and forth, back and forth.

But Smart Alec kept going.

There was so much to do.

She got out her markers

and started drawing on the something.

She drew red and blue and yellow spots.

She drew faces and animals

and big round shapes.

Smart Alec's big sister came outside
to see what was going on.
She said, "What are you building, Alec?"

"I'm building something wonderful,"
said Smart Alec.

Smart Alec's sister said,
"But it looks like it's going to rain."

Smart Alec said, "SHHHHHH!"
So, Smart Alec's big sister stood
and watched while Smart Alec
kept building the wonderful something.

Chapter Four
So Much to Do

Drip, drip, drip.

Smart Alec's big sister said,

"Did anyone feel that?"

And Molly P. Crisp said, "Yeah, I felt that."

And Barney Gavarney said, "Uh oh."

And the Henson twins said, "Uh oh."

And everyone said, "Uh oh, I think
it's starting to rain."

But Smart Alec didn't notice the rain.

She was too busy working on the something.

Smart Alec brought out her bike,
the one with the pink handlebars
and the frilly pink seat.
She dragged it next to the something.
Then she tied it to the bottom
with a ribbon from her hair.

Everyone said, "Come in before you get wet."

Smart Alec said, "Shhhhhh! I'm almost finished."

So everyone hurried inside while Smart Alec kept building the something.

Chapter Five

Almost Done

Drip, drip, drip. The rain dripped down
onto the cardboard boxes, making them all soft
and soggy and wet.

The wind blew very hard.
The incredible something
swayed all over the place.
The big piece of watermelon
started to fall off the end of the stick
that was pointing straight up.

Smart Alec had worked hard.

She was almost done.

There was only one thing left to do.

She sat on her bike and began to pedal.
Then the whole incredible something
came down in a big soggy, soppy mess
of cardboard and raisins and sticks.

And the big piece of watermelon
landed *SPLITCHHH* on Smart Alec's head.

It really was the most incredible something anyone had ever built!